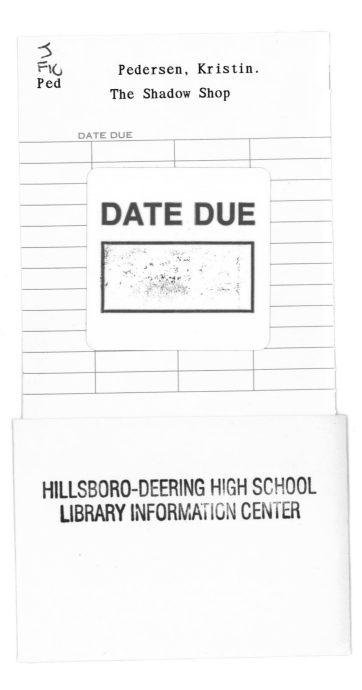

THE SHADOW SHOP

written and illustrated by

Kristin Pedersen

LANDMARK EDITIONS, INC.

P.O. Box 4469 • 1402 Kansas Avenue • Kansas City, Missouri 64127
(816) 241-4919

Dedicated to:
Deborah Hart, who brings sunshine into my life;
Linda Mazur-Jack, who encouraged me to believe in myself;
and to my family.

COPYRIGHT © 1994 BY KRISTIN PEDERSEN

International Standard Book Number: 0-933849-53-2 (LIB.BDG.)

Library of Congress Cataloging-in-Publication Data
Pedersen, Kristin, 1974-
    The shadow shop / written and illustrated by Kristin Pedersen.
        p.   cm.
    Summary: When Thelma McMurty trades her shadow for another one,
she thinks she will live happily ever after.
    ISBN 0-933849-53-2 (lib.bdg. : acid-free paper)
    [1. Shadows—Fiction.   2. Stories in rhyme.]
    I. Title.

PZ8.3.P445Sh   1994
[E]—dc20
                                          94-15366
                                          CIP
                                          AC

Editorial Coordinator: Nancy R. Thatch
Creative Coordinator: David Melton

Printed in the United States of America

Landmark Editions, Inc.
P.O. Box 4469
1402 Kansas Avenue
Kansas City, Missouri 64127
(816) 241-4919

THE SHADOW SHOP

Kristin Pedersen is a "cut-up." With scissors in hand, she cuts sheets of colored paper into all kinds of shapes and sizes. Then she assembles and pastes the pieces together into delightfully witty, cleverly constructed designs and illustrations.

Kristin thinks the cutting and the pasting are fun things to do. And she thinks the mixing and sorting of shapes and textures offer exiting challenges. I think the enjoyment she experiences in creating her extraordinary pictures becomes obvious to those who have the pleasure of seeing them.

As a person and an artist, Kristin has a playful spirit. When we worked together, I always found her to be very "up" and positive. I enjoyed phoning her at her dormitory room at college and hearing the voice on her recording machine announce:

"Hello, you have reached the center of the universe."

When composing illustrations and writing poetry, I have no doubt that Kristin is in the center of a universe — her own universe of creative ideas.

You are about to see and experience a part of Kristin's creative universe. I invite you to join Thelma McMurty and enter THE SHADOW SHOP, where hopes and dreams, and nightmares can be obtained for just one small trade. I think you'll enjoy the adventure.

— David Melton
Creative Coordinator
Landmark Editions, Inc.

Poor Thelma McMurty! She felt like a geek!
Her rough, croaky voice made her sound like a freak.
She sang like a toad croaking deep in a bog.
Her classmates called her, *Thelma the Frog*.

"I'm miserable!" said Thelma. "I feel like a fool.
The whole world's against me. It's terribly cruel.
I'd sing such sweet songs. I'd hit every note,
If only I knew how to clear up my throat."

And she gargled and gurgled, and sprayed her throat well,
Ate peppermint cough drops and fresh minty gel,
But her throat never changed; neither did her voice.
Poor Thelma McMurty was left with no choice . . .

But to go on croaking in her amphibian way.
And it looked like her problem was there to stay,
For her voice sounded worse each time that she spoke —
With a — "RIBBITY! RIBBITY! CROAKETY! CROAK!"

Then . . . one dusty day, it was late in the fall,
As Thelma trudged home so tired of it all,
She walked down an alley and saw a strange store.
She couldn't recall having seen it before.

Its windows were grimy and not very wide,
But Thelma saw something was moving inside.
And the odd little sign on the door made her stop,
For the words read quite simply, *The Shadow Shop*.

So Thelma, as curious as fifty-five cats,
Rapped on the door and peered through the slats.
She reached for the doorknob, but then, with a groan,
The door opened *itself*. Thelma walked in alone.

Hundreds of shadows were hung on the wall!
Her eyes opened wide at the sight of them all.
And stranger than strange, some shadows were moving.
Those shadows were magic — that didn't need proving.

A dancer leaped up and spun through the air!
A soldier marched past, giving Thelma a stare.
A clown blew bubbles of bubbly gum,
And a drummer beat rummedy, dummedy, dum.

Then a scrawny old gypsy came out from the back.
Her bangles and beads gave a click and a clack.
Her smile was warm, but her dark eyes were cold.
And in honeylike tones as rich as pure gold,

She said—"We've been waiting for you, my shadows and I.
We can fix your voice in the blink of an eye.
First you need a new shadow. Let me make the choice.
I'll pick one out now, and you'll have a new voice.

"Take this one," she smiled. "It's a singer, you see.
Just put on this shadow, and a singer you'll be.
If you wear this new shadow, your old voice will change
From croaking to crooning in a magnificent range."

"Will my voice really change?" Thelma asked in a croak.
"Will my singing be gorgeous instead of a joke?"
"Oh, yes," said the gypsy. "Your dream will come true.
So slip on this shadow, and you'll be a new you."

"I'll take it!" said Thelma. "How much does it cost?"
"More than you have, Dearie, but all is not lost.
I'll trade you this shadow for the one you now wear.
Swap your shadow for mine, and you won't have a care."

"I'll trade it!" said Thelma, and so excited was she
That she pulled off her shadow as fast as could be.
And she grabbed her new shadow, slipped it on, pressed it down.
It followed her footsteps as she skipped round and round.

Then she rushed to the mirror that hung on the wall,
Saw a singer for sure, and most astounding of all,
When she opened her mouth, from out of her throat
Flew a perfectly MARVELOUS, GLORIOUS NOTE!

"Oh, wow!" exclaimed Thelma. "Did that come from me?"
"It did," laughed the gypsy, acting pleased as could be.
"Your voice is now lovely; you sound like a star!
Goodbye and good luck, for a singer you are!"

Thelma ran from the shop singing "Hey!" and "Hooray!"
She sang and she sang for the rest of the day.
She sang way up high, and she sang way down low.
She sang really fast, and she sang really slow.

She sang standing up. Then she sang sitting down.
She sang as she cartwheeled her way around town.
She sang on her toes, and she sang on her knees.
And she yodeled the birds right out of the trees.

Then she sang for her parents. She sang for her teachers.
She sang for the kids squished into the bleachers.
When she opened her mouth, she sang non-stop,
From opera, to western, to disco, to pop.

Soon agents appeared, bringing contracts along.
They promised her money for singing each song.
Her voice was on tapes and a smash-hit CD,
And soon she was famous as famous could be.

Her name was on billboards! Her bank account soared!
She sang in the movies and won an award.
Her stretch limousine measured *thirty* feet long,
But . . . then something happened that was terribly wrong.

As the money rolled in, poor Thelma wore out.
She couldn't stop singing or even close her mouth!
Her parents were worried. Her neighbors had a fright
When Thelma struck high C in the middle of the night!

Said Thelma, "This switching of shadows must stop!"
Her limousine drove her back to the shop.
When the door opened wide, Thelma blinked back a tear.
"I need my own shadow!" she cried. "Is it here?"

From out of the gloom, a froggy voice said:
"You've traded your shadow. You're a singer instead.
Your shadow's now mine, and mine it will stay
Forever and ever. Now, get out of my way!"

And from out of that gypsy, a raspy voice spoke —
With a — "RIBBITY! RIBBITY! CROAKETY! CROAK!"

Then the gypsy stepped forward, and in the pale light,
Thelma saw a most horrible, hair-raising sight.
Her shadow was stuck to the gypsy like glue!
But Thelma thought fast. Then she knew what to do.

"You can't have that shadow!" cried Thelma. "It's mine!
That shadow and I share an original design.
Take it off!" ordered Thelma. "You're making me mad!"
The gypsy just shrugged and said, "That's too bad."

"Keep the shadow you have," the old gypsy smiled,
"And leave my shop now, you troublesome child!"
"Never!" shouted Thelma. "I won't leave! I can't!"
Then her voice filled the room with this musical chant:

"Ruffalo, muffalo, alakazoom,
Shadow that's trapped in all of this gloom,
Shadow that's mine, shadow that's me,
Leave that old gypsy and set yourself free!"

Her shadow had heard her! It rose from the ground!
It slipped off the gypsy and darted around.
Then the singer's old shadow slid off in defeat,
And Thelma's own shadow flew straight to her feet.

She grabbed it, put it on, and ran out the door.
She ran and she ran from that terrible store.
Then she rasped and she rumbled as loudly she spoke —
With a — "RIBBITY! RIBBITY! CROAKETY! CROAK!"

Her voice wasn't pretty, but Thelma said, "Hey!
With a croak in my throat, I've got something to say:
From now on strange shadows can stay on the shelf.
I'll keep my own shadow and be my own self."

On some dusty day, should you happen to stop
And peek at the shadows that dance in a shop,
Hold tight to your shadow, whatever you do.
The one that is yours is the best one for you.

BOOKS FOR STUDENTS

— WINNERS OF THE NATIONAL WRITTEN &

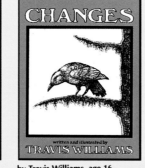

by Benjamin Kendall, age 7
State College, Pennsylvania

When Ben wears his new super-hero costume, he sees Aliens who are from outer space. His attempts to stop the pesky invaders provide loads of laughs. Colorful drawings add to the fun!

Printed Full Color
ISBN 0-933849-42-7

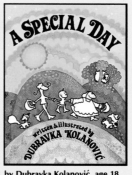

by Steven Shepard, age 13
Great Falls, Virginia

A gripping thriller! When a boy rows his boat to an island to retrieve a stolen knife, he faces threatening fog, treacherous currents, and a sinister lobster-man. Outstanding drawings!

Printed Full Color
ISBN 0-933849-43-5

by Travis Williams, age 16
Sardis, B.C., Canada

A chilling mystery! When a teen-age boy discovers his classmates are missing, he becomes entrapped in a web of conflicting stories, false alibis, and frightening changes. Dramatic drawings!

Printed Two Colors
ISBN 0-933849-44-3

by Dubravka Kolanović, age 18
Savannah, Georgia

Ivan enjoys a wonderful day with his grandparents, a dog, a cat, and a delightful bear that is *always* hungry. Cleverly written, brilliantly illustrated! Little kids love this book!

Printed Full Color
ISBN 0-933849-45-1

by Amy Jones, age 17
Shirley, Arkansas

A whirlwind adventure! An enchanted unicorn helps a young girl rescue her eccentric aunt from the evil Sultan of Zabar. A charming story. Lovely illustrations add a magical glow!

Printed Full Color
ISBN 0-933849-46-X

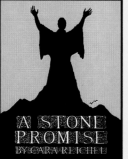

by Cara Reichel, age 15
Rome, Georgia

Elegant and eloquent! A young stonecutter vows to create a great statue for his impoverished village. But his fame almost stops him from fulfilling that promise.

Printed Two Colors
ISBN 0-933849-35-4

by Jonathan Kahn, age 9
Richmond Heights, Ohio

A fascinating nature story! While Patulous, a prairie rattlesnake, searches for food, he must try to avoid the claws and fangs of his own enemies.

Printed Full Color
ISBN 0-933849-36-2

by Jayna Miller, age 19
Zanesville, Ohio

The funniest Halloween ever! When Jammer the Rabbit takes all the treats, his friends get even. Their hilarious scheme includes a haunted house and mounds of chocolate.

Printed Full Color
ISBN 0-933849-37-0

by Lauren Peters, age 7
Kansas City, Missouri

The Christmas that almost wasn't! When Santa Claus takes a vacation, Mrs. Claus and the elves go on strike. Toys aren't made. Cookies aren't baked. Super illustrations.

Printed Full Color
ISBN 0-933849-25-7

by Michael Cain, age 11
Annapolis, Maryland

A glorious tale of adventure! To become a knight, a young man must face a beast in the forest, a spellbinding witch, and a giant bird that guards a magic oval crystal.

Printed Full Color
ISBN 0-933849-26-5

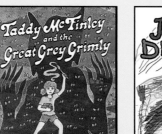

by Heidi Salter, age 19
Berkeley, California

Spooky and wonderful! To save her vivid imagination, a young girl must confront the Great Grey Grimly himself. The narrative is filled with suspense. Vibrant illustrations.

Printed Full Color
ISBN 0-933849-21-4

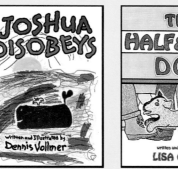

by Dennis Vollmer, age 6
Grove, Oklahoma

A baby whale's curiosity gets him into a lot of trouble. GUINNESS BOOK OF RECORDS lists Dennis as the youngest author/illustrator of a published book.

Printed Full Color
ISBN 0-933849-12-5

by Lisa Gross, age 12
Santa Fe, New Mexico

A touching story of self-esteem! A puppy is laughed at because of his unusual appearance. His search for acceptance is told with sensitivity and humor. Wonderful illustrations.

Printed Full Color
ISBN 0-933849-13-3

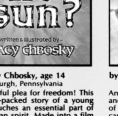

by Stacy Chbosky, age 14
Pittsburgh, Pennsylvania

A powerful plea for freedom! This emotion-packed story of a young slave touches an essential part of the human spirit. Made into a film by Disney Educational Productions.

Printed Full Color
ISBN 0-933849-14-1

by Amy Hagstrom, age 9
Portola, California

An exciting western! When a boy and an old Indian try to save a herd of wild ponies, they discover a lost canyon and see the mystical vision of the Great White Stallion.

Printed Full Color
ISBN 0-933849-15-X

Winning **THE NATIONAL WRITTEN & ILLUSTRATED BY... AWARDS CONTEST** was one of the most important events in my life! I'm very grateful to Landmark Editions for launching my career. The opportunities they gave me and continue to give to other young author/illustrators are invaluable.

—Dav Pilkey, author/illustrator
WORLD WAR WON
and 12 other published books

Share these wonderful books with your students and watch their imaginations soar!

As Rhonda Freese, Teacher, writes:
After I showed the Winning Books to my students, all they wanted to do was WRITE! WRITE! WRITE! and DRAW! DRAW! DRAW!

To motivate and inspire your students, order the Award-Winning Books today! Make sure your students experience all of these important books.

BY STUDENTS!®

ILLUSTRATED BY . . .AWARDS FOR STUDENTS –

by Bonnie-Alise Leggat, age 8
Culpeper, Virginia

Amy J. Kendrick wants to play football, but her mother wants her to become a ballerina. Their clash of wills creates hilarious situations. Clever, delightful illustrations.

Printed Full Color
ISBN 0-933849-39-7

by Lisa Kirsten Butenhoff, age 13
Woodbury, Minnesota

The people of a Russian village face the winter without warm clothes or enough food. Then their lives are improved by a young girl's gifts. A tender story with lovely illustrations.

Printed Full Color
ISBN 0-933849-40-0

by Jennifer Brady, age 17
Columbia, Missouri

When poachers capture a pride of lions, a native boy tries to free the animals. A skillfully told story. Glowing illustrations illuminate this African adventure.

Printed Full Color
ISBN 0-933849-41-9

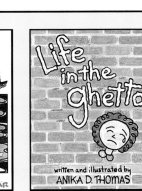

by Aruna Chandrasekhar, age 9
Houston, Texas

A touching and timely story! When the lives of many otters are threatened by a huge oil spill, a group of concerned people come to their rescue. Wonderful illustrations.

Printed Full Color
ISBN 0-933849-33-8

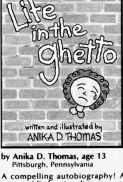

by Anika D. Thomas, age 13
Pittsburgh, Pennsylvania

A compelling autobiography! A young girl's heartrending account of growing up in a tough, inner-city neighborhood. The illustrations match the mood of this gripping story.

Printed Two Colors
ISBN 0-933849-34-6

by Amity Gaige, age 16
Reading, Pennsylvania

A lyrical blend of poetry and photographs! Amity's sensitive poems offer thought-provoking ideas and amusing insights. This lovely book is one to be savored and enjoyed.

Printed Full Color
ISBN 0-933849-27-3

by Adam Moore, age 9
Broken Arrow, Oklahoma

A remarkable true story! When Adam was eight years old, he fell and ran an arrow into his head. With rare insight and humor, he tells of his ordeal and his amazing recovery.

Printed Two Colors
ISBN 0-933849-24-9

by Michael Aushenker, age 19
Ithaca, New York

Chomp! Chomp! When Arthur forgets to feed his goat, the animal eats everything in sight. A very funny story — good to the last bite. The illustrations are terrific.

Printed Full Color
ISBN 0-933849-28-1

by Leslie Ann MacKeen, age 9
Winston-Salem, North Carolina

Loaded with fun and puns! When Jeremiah T. Fitz's car stops running, several animals offer suggestions for fixing it. The results are hilarious. The illustrations are charming.

Printed Full Color
ISBN 0-933849-19-2

by Elizabeth Haidle, age 13
Beaverton, Oregon

A very touching story! The grumpiest Elfkin learns to cherish the friendship of others after he helps an injured snail and befriends an orphaned boy. Absolutely beautiful.

Printed Full Color
ISBN 0-933849-20-6

by Isaac Whitlatch, age 11
Casper, Wyoming

The true confessions of a devout vegetable hater! Isaac tells ways to avoid and dispose of the "slimy green things." His colorful illustrations provide a salad of laughter and mirth.

Printed Full Color
ISBN 0-933849-16-8

by Dav Pilkey, age 19
Cleveland, Ohio

A thought-provoking parable! Two kings halt an arms race and learn to live in peace. This outstanding book launched Dav's professional career. He now has had many books published.

Printed Full Color
ISBN 0-933849-22-2

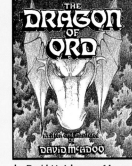

by David McAdoo, age 14
Springfield, Missouri

An exciting intergalactic adventure! In the distant future, a courageous warrior defends a kingdom from a dragon from outer space. Astounding sepia illustrations.

Printed Duotone
ISBN 0-933849-23-0

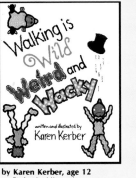

by Karen Kerber, age 12
St. Louis, Missouri

A delightfully playful book! The text is loaded with clever alliterations and gentle humor. Karen's brightly colored illustrations are composed of wiggly and waggly strokes of genius.

Printed Full Color
ISBN 0-933849-29-X

THIS SPACE IS RESERVED FOR A WONDERFUL NEW BOOK

written & illustrated by ONE OF YOUR STUDENTS

The Landmark books are so popular in our school that I had to place them on a special shelf in our library. Now that shelf is always empty.
—Jean Kern, Library Media Specialist

...These books will inspire young writers because of the quality of the works, as well as the young ages of their creators. [They] will prove worthwhile additions for promoting values discussions and encouraging creative writing. —SCHOOL LIBRARY JOURNAL

Having my book published is so exciting! It is fun to be on TV and radio talk shows. And I loved speaking in schools across the country. I enjoy meeting students and encouraging them to write and illustrate their own books.
—Karen Kerber, author/illustrator
WALKING IS WILD, WEIRD & WACKY

Jayna Miller
age 19

Lauren Peter
age 7

Michael Cain
age 11

Heidi Salter
age 19

Amity Gaige
age 16

Dennis Vollmer
age 6

Lisa Gross
age 12

Stacy Chbosky
age 14

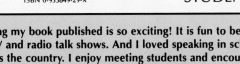
Karen Kerber
age 12

David McAdoo
age 14

THE WINNERS OF THE 1993 NATIONAL
WRITTEN & ILLUSTRATED BY... AWARDS FOR STUDENTS®

FIRST PLACE
6-9 Age Category

FIRST PLACE
10-13 Age Category

FIRST PLACE
14-19 Age Category

Shintaro Maeda, age 8
Wichita, Kansas

Miles MacGregor, age 12
Phoenix, Arizona

Kristin Pedersen, age 18
Etobicoke, Ont., Canada

The birds will not fly in Thomas Raccoon's airshow unless Mr. Eagle approves. And everyone is afraid to talk to Mr. Eagle. So Thomas must face the big grumpy bird alone. Terrific color illustrations add exciting action to the story.

29 Pages, Full Color
ISBN 0-933849-51-6

In a dark, barren land, a young Indian boy dreams of a marvelous Sunflower that can light and warm the earth. To save his tribe from starvation, he must find the flower before it's too late. A beautifully illustrated legend.

29 Pages, Full Color
ISBN 0-933849-52-4

When Thelma McMurty trades her shadow for another one, she thinks she will live happily ever after. But an old gypsy woman knows better. Cleverly told in rhyme. The collage illustrations create a spooky, surreal atmosphere.

29 Pages, Full Color
ISBN 0-933849-53-2

BOOKS FOR STUDENTS BY STUDENTS!

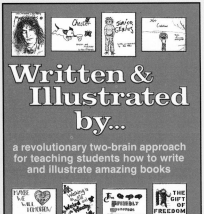

Written & Illustrated by...
by David Melton

This highly acclaimed teacher's manual offers classroom-proven, step-by-step instructions in all aspects of teaching students how to write, illustrate, assemble, and bind original books. Loaded with information and positive approaches that really work. Contains lesson plans, more than 200 illustrations, and suggested adaptations for use at all grade levels — K through college.

The results are dazzling!
Children's Book Review Service, Inc.

WRITTEN & ILLUSTRATED BY... provides a current of enthusiasm, positive thinking and faith in the creative spirit of children. David Melton has the heart of a teacher.
THE READING TEACHER

...an exceptional book! Just browsing through it stimulates excitement for writing.
Joyce E. Juntune, Executive Director
The National Association for Creativity

A "how to" book that really works.
Judy O'Brien, Teacher

Softcover, 96 Pages
ISBN 0-933849-00-1

LANDMARK EDITIONS, INC.
P.O. BOX 4469 • KANSAS CITY, MISSOURI 64127 • (816) 241-4919